THE PROPHET

Kahlil Gibran

ISBN 9781794681354

CONTENTS

THE PROPHET

Almustafa, the chosen and the beloved,
who was a dawn unto his own
day, had waited twelve years in the city
of Orphalese for his ship that was to
return and bear him back to the isle of
his birth.

And in the twelfth year, on the seventh
day of Ielool, the month of reaping, he
climbed the hill without the city walls
and looked seaward; and he beheld his
ship coming with the mist.

Then the gates of his heart were flung
open, and his joy flew far over the sea.
And he closed his eyes and prayed in the
silences of his soul.

. . .

But as he descended the hill, a sadness
came upon him, and he thought in his
heart:

How shall I go in peace and without
sorrow? Nay, not without a wound in the
spirit shall I leave this city. Long
were the days of pain I have spent
within its walls, and long were the
nights of aloneness; and who can depart
from his pain and his aloneness without
regret?

Too many fragments of the spirit have I
scattered in these streets, and too many
are the children of my longing that walk
naked among these hills, and I cannot
withdraw from them without a burden and
an ache.

It is not a garment I cast off this day, but a skin that I tear with my own hands.

Nor is it a thought I leave behind me, but a heart made sweet with hunger and with thirst.

. . .

Yet I cannot tarry longer.

The sea that calls all things unto her calls me, and I must embark.

For to stay, though the hours burn in the night, is to freeze and crystallize and be bound in a mould.

Fain would I take with me all that is here. But how shall I?

A voice cannot carry the tongue and the lips that gave it wings. Alone must it seek the ether.

And alone and without his nest shall the eagle fly across the sun.

. . .

Now when he reached the foot of the hill, he turned again towards the sea, and he saw his ship approaching the harbour, and upon her prow the mariners, the men of his own land.

And his soul cried out to them, and he said:

Sons of my ancient mother, you riders of
the tides,

How often have you sailed in my dreams.
And now you come in my awakening, which
is my deeper dream.

Ready am I to go, and my eagerness with
sails full set awaits the wind.

Only another breath will I breathe in
this still air, only another loving look
cast backward,

And then I shall stand among you, a
seafarer among seafarers. And you,
vast sea, sleepless mother,

Who alone are peace and freedom to the
river and the stream,

Only another winding will this stream
make, only another murmur in this glade,

And then shall I come to you, a
boundless drop to a boundless ocean.

. . .

And as he walked he saw from afar men
and women leaving their fields and their
vineyards and hastening towards the city
gates.

And he heard their voices calling his
name, and shouting from field to field
telling one another of the coming of his
ship.

And he said to himself:

Shall the day of parting be the day of

gathering?

And shall it be said that my eve was in truth my dawn?

And what shall I give unto him who has left his plough in midfurrow, or to him who has stopped the wheel of his winepress? Shall my heart become a tree heavy-laden with fruit that I may gather and give unto them?

And shall my desires flow like a fountain that I may fill their cups?

Am I a harp that the hand of the mighty may touch me, or a flute that his breath may pass through me?

A seeker of silences am I, and what treasure have I found in silences that I may dispense with confidence?

If this is my day of harvest, in what fields have I sowed the seed, and in what unremembered seasons?

If this indeed be the hour in which I lift up my lantern, it is not my flame that shall burn therein.

Empty and dark shall I raise my lantern,

And the guardian of the night shall fill it with oil and he shall light it also.

. . .

These things he said in words. But much in his heart remained unsaid. For he himself could not speak his deeper secret.

. . .

And when he entered into the city all
the people came to meet him, and they
were crying out to him as with one
voice.

And the elders of the city stood forth
and said:

Go not yet away from us.

A noontide have you been in our
twilight, and your youth has given us
dreams to dream.

No stranger are you among us, nor
a guest, but our son and our dearly
beloved.

Suffer not yet our eyes to hunger for
your face.

. . .

And the priests and the priestesses said
unto him:

Let not the waves of the sea separate us
now, and the years you have spent in our
midst become a memory.

You have walked among us a spirit,
and your shadow has been a light
upon our faces.

Much have we loved you. But speechless
was our love, and with veils has it been
veiled.

Yet now it cries aloud unto you, and

would stand revealed before you.

And ever has it been that love knows
not its own depth until the hour of
separation.

. . .

And others came also and entreated him.
But he answered them not. He only bent
his head; and those who stood near saw
his tears falling upon his breast.

And he and the people proceeded towards
the great square before the temple.

And there came out of the sanctuary a
woman whose name was Almitra. And she was a seeress.

And he looked upon her with exceeding
tenderness, for it was she who had first
sought and believed in him when he had
been but a day in their city. And
she hailed him, saying:

Prophet of God, in quest of the
uttermost, long have you searched the
distances for your ship.

And now your ship has come, and you must
needs
go.

Deep is your longing for the land of
your memories and the dwelling place
of your greater desires; and our love
would not bind you nor our needs hold
you.

Yet this we ask ere you leave us, that
you speak to us and give us of your
truth.

And we will give it unto our children,
and they unto their children, and it
shall not perish.

In your aloneness you have watched with our days, and in your
wakefulness you have listened to the weeping and the
laughter of our sleep.

Now therefore disclose us to ourselves,
and tell us all that has been shown
you of that which is between birth and
death.

. . .

And he answered,

People of Orphalese, of what can I
speak save of that which is even now
moving within your souls?

. . . . . .

Then said Almitra, Speak to us of
Love.

And he raised his head and looked upon
the people, and there fell a stillness
upon them. And with a great voice he
said:

When love beckons to you, follow him,

Though his ways are hard and steep.

And when his wings enfold you yield to
him,

Though the sword hidden among his
pinions may wound you.

And when he speaks to you believe in
him,

Though his voice may shatter your dreams
as the north wind lays waste the garden.

For even as love crowns you so shall
he crucify you. Even as he is for your
growth so is he for your pruning.

Even as he ascends to your height and
caresses your tenderest branches
that quiver in the sun,

So shall he descend to your roots and
shake them in their clinging to the
earth.

. . .

Like sheaves of corn he gathers you unto himself.

He threshes you to make you naked.

He sifts you to free you from your
husks.

He grinds you to whiteness.

He kneads you until you are pliant;

And then he assigns you to his sacred
fire, that you may become sacred bread
for God's sacred feast.

. . .

All these things shall love do unto you
that you may know the secrets of your
heart, and in that knowledge become a
fragment of Life's heart.

But if in your fear you would seek only
love's peace and love's pleasure,

Then it is better for you that you
cover your nakedness and pass out of
love's threshing-floor,

Into the seasonless world where you
shall laugh, but not all of your
laughter, and weep, but not all of your
tears.

. . .

Love gives naught but itself and takes
naught but from itself.

Love possesses not nor would it be
possessed;

For love is sufficient unto love.

When you love you should not say, "God
is in my heart," but rather, "I am in
the heart of God."

And think not you can direct the course
of love, for love, if it finds you
worthy, directs your course.

Love has no other desire but to fulfil
itself.

But if you love and must needs have
desires, let these be your desires:

To melt and be like a running brook that
sings its melody to the night. To
know the pain of too much tenderness.

To be wounded by your own understanding
of love;

And to bleed willingly and joyfully.

To wake at dawn with a winged heart and
give thanks for another day of loving;

To rest at the noon hour and meditate
love's ecstasy;

To return home at eventide with
gratitude;

And then to sleep with a prayer for
the beloved in your heart and a song of
praise upon your lips.

. . . . . .

Then Almitra spoke again and said,
And what of *Marriage* master?

And he answered saying:

You were born together, and together you
shall be forevermore.

You shall be together when the white
wings of death scatter your days.

Aye, you shall be together even in the
silent memory of God.

But let there be spaces in your
togetherness,

And let the winds of the heavens dance
between you.

. . .

Love one another, but make not a bond of
love:

Let it rather be a moving sea between
the shores of your souls.

Fill each other's cup but drink not from
one cup.

Give one another of your bread but eat
not from the same loaf. Sing and
dance together and be joyous, but let
each one of you be alone,

Even as the strings of a lute are alone
though they quiver with the same music.

. . .

Give your hearts, but not into each
other's keeping.

For only the hand of Life can contain
your hearts.

And stand together yet not too near
together:

For the pillars of the temple stand
apart,

And the oak tree and the cypress grow
not in each other's shadow.

. . . . . .

And a woman who held a babe
against her bosom said, Speak to us of
Children.

And he said:

Your children are not your children.

They are the sons and daughters of
Life's longing for itself.

They come through you but not from you,

And though they are with you yet they
belong not to you.

. . .

You may give them your love but not your
thoughts,

For they have their own thoughts.

You may house their bodies but not their
souls,

For their souls dwell in the house of
tomorrow, which you cannot visit, not
even in your dreams.

You may strive to be like them, but seek
not to make them like you. For
life goes not backward nor tarries with
yesterday.

You are the bows from which your
children as living arrows are sent
forth.

The archer sees the mark upon the path
of the infinite, and He bends you with
His might that His arrows may go swift
and far.

Let your bending in the Archer's hand be
for gladness;

For even as he loves the arrow that
flies, so He loves also the bow that is
stable.

. . . . . .

Then said a rich man, Speak to us of
Giving.

And he answered:

You give but little when you give of
your possessions.

It is when you give of yourself that you
truly give.

For what are your possessions but things
you keep and guard for fear you may need
them tomorrow?

And tomorrow, what shall tomorrow bring
to the overprudent dog burying bones
in the trackless sand as he follows the
pilgrims to the holy city?

And what is fear of need but need
itself?

Is not dread of thirst when your well is
full, the thirst that is unquenchable?

There are those who give little of the
much which they have--and they give
it for recognition and their hidden
desire makes their gifts unwholesome.

And there are those who have little and
give it all.

These are the believers in life and
the bounty of life, and their coffer is
never empty.

There are those who give with joy, and

that joy is their reward.

And there are those who give with pain,
and that pain is their baptism.

And there are those who give and know
not pain in giving, nor do they seek
joy, nor give with mindfulness of
virtue;

They give as in yonder valley the myrtle
breathes its fragrance into space.

Through the hands of such as these God
speaks, and from behind their eyes He
smiles upon the earth.

It is well to give when asked, but it
is better to give unasked, through
understanding;

And to the open-handed the search for
one who shall receive is joy greater
than giving.

And is there aught you would withhold?

All you have shall someday be given;

Therefore give now, that the season
of giving may be yours and not your
inheritors'.

You often say, "I would give, but only
to the deserving."

The trees in your orchard say not so,
nor the flocks in your pasture.

They give that they may live, for to
withhold is to perish.

Surely he who is worthy to receive his
days and his nights, is worthy of all
else from you.

And he who has deserved to drink from
the ocean of life deserves to fill his
cup from your little stream.

And what desert greater shall there be,
than that which lies in the courage
and the confidence, nay the charity, of
receiving?

And who are you that men should rend
their bosom and unveil their pride,
that you may see their worth naked and
their pride unabashed?

See first that you yourself deserve to
be a giver, and an instrument of giving.

For in truth it is life that gives unto
life--while you, who deem yourself a
giver, are but a witness.

And you receivers--and you are
all receivers--assume no weight of
gratitude, lest you lay a yoke upon
yourself and upon him who gives.

Rather rise together with the giver on
his gifts as on wings;

For to be overmindful of your debt, is
to doubt his generosity who has the
freehearted earth for mother, and God
for father.

. . . . . .

Then an old man, a keeper of an

inn, said, Speak to us of *Eating and Drinking*.

And he said:

Would that you could live on the fragrance of the earth, and like an air plant be sustained by the light.

But since you must kill to eat, and rob the newly born of its mother's milk to quench your thirst, let it then be an act of worship,

And let your board stand an altar on which the pure and the innocent of forest and plain are sacrificed for that which is purer and still more innocent in man.

. . .

When you kill a beast say to him in your heart,

"By the same power that slays you, I too am slain; and I too shall be consumed. For the law that delivered you into my hand shall deliver me into a mightier hand.

Your blood and my blood is naught but the sap that feeds the tree of heaven."

. . .

And when you crush an apple with your teeth, say to it in your heart,

"Your seeds shall live in my body,

And the buds of your tomorrow shall

blossom in my heart,

And your fragrance shall be my breath,
And together we shall rejoice through
all the seasons."

. . .

And in the autumn, when you gather
the grapes of your vineyards for the
winepress, say in your heart,

"I too am a vineyard, and my fruit shall
be gathered for the winepress,

And like new wine I shall be kept in
eternal vessels."

And in winter, when you draw the wine,
let there be in your heart a song
for each cup;

And let there be in the song a
remembrance for the autumn days, and for
the vineyard, and for the winepress.

. . .

Then a ploughman said, Speak
to us of *Work*.

And he answered, saying:

You work that you may keep pace with the
earth and the soul of the earth.

For to be idle is to become a stranger
unto the seasons, and to step out of
life's procession, that marches in
majesty and proud submission towards the
infinite.

When you work you are a flute through
whose heart the whispering of the hours
turns to music.

Which of you would be a reed, dumb and
silent, when all else sings together in
unison?

Always you have been told that work is a curse and labor a
misfortune.

But I say to you that when you work you
fulfil a part of earth's furthest dream,
assigned to you when that dream was
born,

And in keeping yourself with labor you
are in truth loving life,

And to love life through labor is to be
intimate with life's inmost secret.

. . .

But if you in your pain call birth an
affliction and the support of the flesh
a curse written upon your brow, then I
answer that naught but the sweat of
your brow shall wash away that which is
written.

You have been told also that life is
darkness, and in your weariness you echo
what was said by the weary.

And I say that life is indeed darkness
'save when there is urge,

And all urge is blind save when there is
knowledge,

And all knowledge is vain save when

there is work,

And all work is empty save when there is love;

And when you work with love you bind
yourself to yourself, and to one
another, and to God.

. . .

And what is it to work with love?

It is to weave the cloth with threads
drawn from your heart, even as if your
beloved were to wear that cloth.

It is to build a house with affection,
even as if your beloved were to dwell in
that house.

It is to sow seeds with tenderness and
reap the harvest with joy, even as if
your beloved were to eat the fruit.

It is to charge all things you fashion
with a breath of your own spirit,

And to know that all the blessed dead
are standing about you and watching.

Often have I heard you say, as if
speaking in sleep, "He who works in
marble, and finds the shape of his own
soul in the stone, is nobler than he who
ploughs the soil. And he who seizes
the rainbow to lay it on a cloth in the
likeness of man, is more than he who
makes the sandals for our feet."

But I say, not in sleep but in the
overwakefulness of noontide, that the
wind speaks not more sweetly to the

giant oaks than to the least of all the
blades of grass;

And he alone is great who turns the
voice of the wind into a song made
sweeter by his own loving.

. . .

Work is love made visible.

And if you cannot work with love but
only with distaste, it is better that
you should leave your work and sit at
the gate of the temple and take alms of
those who work with joy.

For if you bake bread with indifference,
you bake a bitter bread that feeds but
half man's hunger.

And if you grudge the crushing of the
grapes, your grudge distils a poison in
the wine. And if you sing though as
angels, and love not the singing, you
muffle man's ears to the voices of the
day and the voices of the night.

. . . . . .

Then a woman said, Speak to us of
Joy and Sorrow.

And he answered:

Your joy is your sorrow unmasked.

And the selfsame well from which your
laughter rises was oftentimes filled
with your tears.

And how else can it be?

The deeper that sorrow carves into your being, the more joy you can contain.

Is not the cup that holds your wine the very cup that was burned in the potter's oven?

And is not the lute that soothes your spirit, the very wood that was hollowed with knives?

When you are joyous, look deep into your heart and you shall find it is only that which has given you sorrow that is giving you joy.

When you are sorrowful look again in your heart, and you shall see that in truth you are weeping for that which has been your delight.

. . .

Some of you say, "Joy is greater than sorrow," and others say, "Nay, sorrow is the greater."

But I say unto you, they are inseparable.

Together they come, and when one sits alone with you at your board, remember that the other is asleep upon your bed.

Verily you are suspended like scales between your sorrow and your joy.

Only when you are empty are you at standstill and balanced.

When the treasure-keeper lifts you to

weigh his gold and his silver, needs
must your joy or your sorrow rise or
fall.

. . . . . .

Then a mason came forth and said,
Speak to us of *Houses*.

And he answered and said:

Build of your imaginings a bower in the
wilderness ere you build a house within
the city walls.

For even as you have home-comings in
your twilight, so has the wanderer in
you, the ever distant and alone.

Your house is your larger body.

It grows in the sun and sleeps in the
stillness of the night; and it is not
dreamless. Does not your house dream?
and dreaming, leave the city for grove
or hilltop?

Would that I could gather your houses
into my hand, and like a sower scatter
them in forest and meadow.

Would the valleys were your streets, and
the green paths your alleys, that you
might seek one another through
vineyards, and come with the fragrance
of the earth in your garments.

But these things are not yet to be.

In their fear your forefathers gathered
you too near together. And that fear
shall endure a little longer. A little

longer shall your city walls separate
your hearths from your fields.

. . .

And tell me, people of Orphalese, what
have you in these houses? And what is it
you guard with fastened doors?

Have you peace, the quiet urge that
reveals your power?

Have you remembrances, the glimmering
arches that span the summits of the
mind?

Have you beauty, that leads the heart
from things fashioned of wood and stone
to the holy mountain?

Tell me, have you these in your houses?

Or have you only comfort, and the lust
for comfort, that stealthy thing that
enters the house a guest, and then
becomes a host, and then a master?

. . .

Ay, and it becomes a tamer, and with
hook and scourge makes puppets of your larger desires.

Though its hands are silken, its heart
is of iron.

It lulls you to sleep only to stand by
your bed and jeer at the dignity of the
flesh.

It makes mock of your sound senses, and lays them in thistledown
like fragile
vessels.

Verily the lust for comfort murders
the passion of the soul, and then walks
grinning in the funeral.

But you, children of space, you restless
in rest, you shall not be trapped nor
tamed.

Your house shall be not an anchor but a
mast.

It shall not be a glistening film that covers a wound, but an eyelid
that
guards the eye.

You shall not fold your wings that you
may pass through doors, nor bend your
heads that they strike not against a
ceiling, nor fear to breathe lest walls
should crack and fall down.

You shall not dwell in tombs made by the
dead for the living.

And though of magnificence and
splendor, your house shall not hold
your secret nor shelter your longing.

For that which is boundless in you
abides in the mansion of the sky, whose
door is the morning mist, and whose
windows are the songs and the silences
of night.

. . . . . .

And the weaver said, Speak to us of
Clothes.

And he answered:

Your clothes conceal much of your
beauty, yet they hide not the
unbeautiful.

And though you seek in garments the
freedom of privacy you may find in them
a harness and a chain.

Would that you could meet the sun and
the wind with more of your skin and less
of your raiment,

For the breath of life is in the
sunlight and the hand of life is in the
wind.

Some of you say, "It is the north wind
who has woven the clothes we wear."

And I say, Ay, it was the north wind,

But shame was his loom, and the
softening of the sinews was his thread.

And when his work was done he laughed in
the forest. Forget not that modesty
is for a shield against the eye of the
unclean.

And when the unclean shall be no more,
what were modesty but a fetter and a
fouling of the mind?

And forget not that the earth delights
to feel your bare feet and the winds
long to play with your hair.

. . . . . .

And a merchant said, Speak to us of
Buying and Selling.

And he answered and said:

To you the earth yields her fruit, and you shall not want if you but know how to fill your hands.

It is in exchanging the gifts of the earth that you shall find abundance and be satisfied.

Yet unless the exchange be in love and kindly justice, it will but lead some to greed and others to hunger.

When in the market place you toilers of the sea and fields and vineyards meet the weavers and the potters and the gatherers of spices,--

Invoke then the master spirit of the earth, to come into your midst and sanctify the scales and the reckoning that weighs value against value. And suffer not the barren-handed to take part in your transactions, who would sell their words for your labor.

To such men you should say,

"Come with us to the field, or go with our brothers to the sea and cast your net;

For the land and the sea shall be bountiful to you even as to us."

. . .

And if there come the singers and the dancers and the flute players,--buy of their gifts also.

For they too are gatherers of fruit and
frankincense, and that which they bring,
though fashioned of dreams, is raiment
and food for your soul.

And before you leave the market place,
see that no one has gone his way with
empty hands.

For the master spirit of the earth shall
not sleep peacefully upon the wind
till the needs of the least of you are
satisfied.

. . . . . .

Then one of the judges of the city
stood forth and said, Speak to us of
Crime and Punishment.

And he answered, saying:

It is when your spirit goes wandering
upon the wind,

That you, alone and unguarded, commit
a wrong unto others and therefore unto
yourself.

And for that wrong committed must you
knock and wait a while unheeded at the
gate of the blessed.

Like the ocean is your god-self;

It remains forever undefiled.

And like the ether it lifts but the
winged.

Even like the sun is your god-self;

It knows not the ways of the mole nor
seeks it the holes of the serpent.
But your god-self dwells not alone
in your being.

Much in you is still man, and much in
you is not yet man,

But a shapeless pygmy that walks asleep
in the mist searching for its own
awakening.

And of the man in you would I now speak.

For it is he and not your god-self nor
the pygmy in the mist, that knows crime
and the punishment of crime.

. . .

Oftentimes have I heard you speak of one who commits a wrong as
though he were not one of you, but a stranger unto you and an
intruder upon your world.

But I say that even as the holy and the
righteous cannot rise beyond the highest
which is in each one of you,

So the wicked and the weak cannot fall
lower than the lowest which is in you
also.

And as a single leaf turns not yellow
but with the silent knowledge of the
whole tree,

So the wrong-doer cannot do wrong without the hidden will of you
all.

Like a procession you walk together
towards your god-self.

You are the way and the wayfarers.

And when one of you falls down he falls
for those behind him, a caution against
the stumbling stone.

Ay, and he falls for those ahead of him,
who though faster and surer of foot, yet
removed not the stumbling stone.

And this also, though the word lie heavy
upon your hearts:

The murdered is not unaccountable for
his own murder,

And the robbed is not blameless in being
robbed.

The righteous is not innocent of the
deeds of the wicked,

And the white-handed is not clean in the
doings of the felon.

Yea, the guilty is oftentimes the victim
of the injured,

And still more often the condemned is
the burden bearer for the guiltless
and unblamed.

You cannot separate the just from the
unjust and the good from the wicked;

For they stand together before the face
of the sun even as the black thread and
the white are woven together.

And when the black thread breaks, the
weaver shall look into the whole cloth,
and he shall examine the loom also.

. . .

If any of you would bring to judgment
the unfaithful wife,

Let him also weigh the heart of her
husband in scales, and measure his soul
with measurements.

And let him who would lash the offender
look unto the spirit of the offended.

And if any of you would punish in the
name of righteousness and lay the ax
unto the evil tree, let him see to its
roots;

And verily he will find the roots of the
good and the bad, the fruitful and the
fruitless, all entwined together in
the silent heart of the earth.

And you judges who would be just,

What judgment pronounce you upon him
who though honest in the flesh yet is a
thief in spirit?

What penalty lay you upon him who slays
in the flesh yet is himself slain in the
spirit?

And how prosecute you him who in action is a deceiver and an
oppressor,

Yet who also is aggrieved and outraged?

. . .

And how shall you punish those whose
remorse is already greater than their

misdeeds?

Is not remorse the justice which is administered by that very law which you would fain serve?

Yet you cannot lay remorse upon the innocent nor lift it from the heart of the guilty.

Unbidden shall it call in the night, that men may wake and gaze upon themselves. And you who would understand justice, how shall you unless you look upon all deeds in the fullness of light?

Only then shall you know that the erect and the fallen are but one man standing in twilight between the night of his pygmy-self and the day of his god-self, And that the corner-stone of the temple is not higher than the lowest stone in its foundation.

. . . . . .

Then a lawyer said, But what of our *Laws*, master?

And he answered:

You delight in laying down laws,

Yet you delight more in breaking them.

Like children playing by the ocean who build sand-towers with constancy and then destroy them with laughter.

But while you build your sand-towers the ocean brings more sand to the shore,

And when you destroy them the ocean
laughs with you.

Verily the ocean laughs always with the
innocent.

But what of those to whom life is not
an ocean, and man-made laws are not
sand-towers,

But to whom life is a rock, and the law
a chisel with which they would carve it
in their own likeness? What of the
cripple who hates dancers?

What of the ox who loves his yoke and
deems the elk and deer of the forest
stray and vagrant things?

What of the old serpent who cannot shed
his skin, and calls all others naked and
shameless?

And of him who comes early to the
wedding-feast, and when over-fed and
tired goes his way saying that all
feasts are violation and all feasters
lawbreakers?

. . .

What shall I say of these save that
they too stand in the sunlight, but with
their backs to the sun?

They see only their shadows, and their
shadows are their laws.

And what is the sun to them but a caster
of shadows?

And what is it to acknowledge the
laws but to stoop down and trace their
shadows upon the earth?

But you who walk facing the sun, what
images drawn on the earth can hold
you?

You who travel with the wind, what
weather-vane shall direct your course?

What man's law shall bind you if you
break your yoke but upon no man's prison door?

What laws shall you fear if you dance
but stumble against no man's iron
chains?

And who is he that shall bring you to
judgment if you tear off your garment
yet leave it in no man's path?

. . .

People of Orphalese, you can muffle the
drum, and you can loosen the strings
of the lyre, but who shall command the
skylark not to sing?

. . . . . .

And an orator said, Speak to us of
Freedom.

And he answered:

At the city gate and by your fireside
I have seen you prostrate yourself and
worship your own freedom,

Even as slaves humble themselves before a tyrant and praise him
though he slays them.

Ay, in the grove of the temple and in
the shadow of the citadel I have seen
the freest among you wear their freedom
as a yoke and a handcuff.

And my heart bled within me; for you
can only be free when even the desire
of seeking freedom becomes a harness
to you, and when you cease to speak of
freedom as a goal and a fulfilment.

You shall be free indeed when your
days are not without a care nor your
nights without a want and a grief,

But rather when these things girdle your
life and yet you rise above them naked
and unbound.

. . .

And how shall you rise beyond your days
and nights unless you break the
chains which you at the dawn of your
understanding have fastened around your
noon hour?

In truth that which you call freedom is
the strongest of these chains, though
its links glitter in the sun and dazzle
your eyes.

And what is it but fragments of your
own self you would discard that you may become free?

If it is an unjust law you would
abolish, that law was written with your
own hand upon your own forehead.

You cannot erase it by burning your law
books nor by washing the foreheads of

your judges, though you pour the sea
upon them.

And if it is a despot you would
dethrone, see first that his throne
erected within you is destroyed.

For how can a tyrant rule the free and
the proud, but for a tyranny in their
own freedom and a shame in their own
pride?

And if it is a care you would cast off,
that cart has been chosen by you rather
than imposed upon you.

And if it is a fear you would dispel,
the seat of that fear is in your heart
and not in the hand of the feared.

. . .

Verily all things move within your being
in constant half embrace, the desired
and the dreaded, the repugnant and the
cherished, the pursued and that which
you would escape.

These things move within you as lights
and shadows in pairs that cling.

And when the shadow fades and is no
more, the light that lingers becomes a
shadow to another light.

And thus your freedom when it loses its
fetters becomes itself the fetter of a
greater freedom.

. . . . . .

And the priestess spoke again

and said: Speak to us of *Reason and Passion.*

And he answered, saying:

Your soul is oftentimes a battlefield,
upon which your reason and your judgment wage war against your
passion and your appetite.

Would that I could be the peacemaker in
your soul, that I might turn the discord
and the rivalry of your elements into
oneness and melody.

But how shall I, unless you yourselves
be also the peacemakers, nay, the lovers
of all your elements?

Your reason and your passion are the
rudder and the sails of your seafaring
soul.

If either your sails or your rudder be
broken, you can but toss and drift,
or else be held at a standstill in
mid-seas. For reason, ruling alone,
is a force confining; and passion,
unattended, is a flame that burns to its
own destruction.

Therefore let your soul exalt your
reason to the height of passion, that it
may sing;

And let it direct your passion with
reason, that your passion may live
through its own daily resurrection,
and like the phoenix rise above its own
ashes.

. . .

I would have you consider your judgment
and your appetite even as you would two loved guests in your
house.

Surely you would not honour one guest
above the other; for he who is more
mindful of one loses the love and the
faith of both

Among the hills, when you sit in the
cool shade of the white poplars, sharing
the peace and serenity of distant fields
and meadows--then let your heart say in
silence, "God rests in reason."

And when the storm comes, and the
mighty wind shakes the forest,
and thunder and lightning proclaim the
majesty of the sky,--then let your heart
say in awe, "God moves in passion."

And since you are a breath in God's
sphere, and a leaf in God's forest, you
too should rest in reason and move in
passion.

. . . . . .

And a woman spoke, saying, Tell us
of *Pain*.

And he said:

Your pain is the breaking of the shell
that encloses your understanding.

Even as the stone of the fruit must
break, that its heart may stand in the
sun, so must you know pain.

And could you keep your heart in wonder
at the daily miracles of your life, your

pain would not seem less wondrous than
your joy;

And you would accept the seasons of your heart, even as you have
always accepted the seasons that pass over your fields.

And you would watch with serenity
through the winters of your grief.

Much of your pain is self-chosen.

It is the bitter potion by which the
physician within you heals your sick
self.

Therefore trust the physician, and drink
his remedy in silence and tranquillity:
For his hand, though heavy and hard, is
guided by the tender hand of the Unseen,
And the cup he brings, though it burn
your lips, has been fashioned of the
clay which the Potter has moistened with
His own sacred tears.

. . . . . .

And a man said, Speak to us of
Self-Knowledge.

And he answered, saying:

Your hearts know in silence the secrets
of the days and the nights.

But your ears thirst for the sound of
your heart's knowledge.

You would know in words that which you have always known in
thought.

You would touch with your fingers the
naked body of your dreams.

And it is well you should.

The hidden well-spring of your soul must needs rise and run murmuring to the sea;

And the treasure of your infinite depths would be revealed to your eyes.

But let there be no scales to weigh your unknown treasure;

And seek not the depths of your knowledge with staff or sounding line.

For self is a sea boundless and measureless.

. . .

Say not, "I have found the truth," but rather, "I have found a truth."

Say not, "I have found the path of the soul." Say rather, "I have met the soul walking upon my path."

For the soul walks upon all paths.

The soul walks not upon a line, neither does it grow like a reed.

The soul unfolds itself, like a lotus of countless petals.

. . . . . .

Then said a teacher, Speak to us of *Teaching*.

And he said:

"No man can reveal to you aught but that which already lies half asleep in the dawning of your knowledge.

The teacher who walks in the shadow of the temple, among his followers, gives not of his wisdom but rather of his faith and his lovingness.

If he is indeed wise he does not bid you enter the house of his wisdom, but rather leads you to the threshold of your own mind.

The astronomer may speak to you of his understanding of space, but he cannot give you his understanding.

The musician may sing to you of the rhythm which is in all space, but he cannot give you the ear which arrests the rhythm nor the voice that echoes it. And he who is versed in the science of numbers can tell of the regions of weight and measure, but he cannot conduct you thither.

For the vision of one man lends not its wings to another man.

And even as each one of you stands alone in God's knowledge, so must each one of you be alone in his knowledge of God and in his understanding of the earth.

. . . . . .

And a youth said, Speak to us of *Friendship*.

And he answered, saying:

Your friend is your needs answered.

He is your field which you sow with love
and reap with thanksgiving.

And he is your board and your fireside.

For you come to him with your hunger,
and you seek him for peace.

When your friend speaks his mind you
fear not the "nay" in your own mind, nor
do you withhold the "ay."

And when he is silent your heart ceases
not to listen to his heart;

For without words, in friendship, all
thoughts, all desires, all expectations
are born and shared, with joy that is
unacclaimed.

When you part from your friend, you
grieve not;

For that which you love most in him
may be clearer in his absence, as the
mountain to the climber is clearer
from the plain. And let there be no
purpose in friendship save the deepening
of the spirit.

For love that seeks aught but the
disclosure of its own mystery is not
love but a net cast forth: and only the
unprofitable is caught.

. . .

And let your best be for your friend.

If he must know the ebb of your tide,
let him know its flood also.

For what is your friend that you should
seek him with hours to kill?

Seek him always with hours to live.

For it is his to fill your need, but not
your emptiness.

And in the sweetness of friendship
let there be laughter, and sharing of
pleasures.

For in the dew of little things
the heart finds its morning and is
refreshed.

. . . . . .

And then a scholar said, Speak of
Talking.

And he answered, saying:

You talk when you cease to be at peace
with your thoughts;

And when you can no longer dwell in the
solitude of your heart you live in your
lips, and sound is a diversion and a
pastime.

And in much of your talking, thinking is
half murdered.

For thought is a bird of space, that in
a cage of words may indeed unfold its
wings but cannot fly.

There are those among you who seek the

talkative through fear of being alone.

The silence of aloneness reveals to
their eyes their naked selves and they
would escape.

And there are those who talk, and
without knowledge or forethought reveal
a truth which they themselves do not
understand.

And there are those who have the truth
within them, but they tell it not in
words.

In the bosom of such as these the spirit
dwells in rhythmic silence.

. . .

When you meet your friend on the
roadside or in the market place, let the
spirit in you move your lips and direct
your tongue.

Let the voice within your voice speak to
the ear of his ear;

For his soul will keep the truth of
your heart as the taste of the wine is
remembered

When the colour is forgotten and the
vessel is no more.

. . . . . .

And an astronomer said, Master, what
of *Time*?

And he answered:

You would measure time the measureless
and the immeasurable.

You would adjust your conduct and
even direct the course of your spirit
according to hours and seasons.

Of time you would make a stream upon
whose bank you would sit and watch its
flowing.

Yet the timeless in you is aware of
life's timelessness,

And knows that yesterday is but today's
memory and tomorrow is today's dream.

And that that which sings and
contemplates in you is still dwelling
within the bounds of that first moment
which scattered the stars into space.
Who among you does not feel that his
power to love is boundless?

And yet who does not feel that very
love, though boundless, encompassed
within the centre of his being, and
moving not from love thought to love
thought, nor from love deeds to other
love deeds?

And is not time even as love is,
undivided and paceless?

. . .

But if in your thought you must measure
time into seasons, let each season
encircle all the other seasons,

And let today embrace the past with
remembrance and the future with longing.

. . . . . .

And one of the elders of the city
said, Speak to us of *Good and Evil*.

And he answered:

Of the good in you I can speak, but not
of the evil.

For what is evil but good tortured by
its own hunger and thirst?

Verily when good is hungry it seeks food
even in dark caves, and when it thirsts
it drinks even of dead waters.

You are good when you are one with
yourself.

Yet when you are not one with yourself
you are not evil.

For a divided house is not a den of
thieves; it is only a divided house.

And a ship without rudder may wander
aimlessly among perilous isles yet sink
not to the bottom. You are good when
you strive to give of yourself.

Yet you are not evil when you seek gain
for yourself.

For when you strive for gain you are
but a root that clings to the earth and
sucks at her breast.

Surely the fruit cannot say to the root,
"Be like me, ripe and full and ever
giving of your abundance."

45

For to the fruit giving is a need, as
receiving is a need to the root.

. . .

You are good when you are fully awake in
your speech,

Yet you are not evil when you sleep
while your tongue staggers without
purpose.

And even stumbling speech may strengthen
a weak tongue.

You are good when you walk to your goal
firmly and with bold steps.

Yet you are not evil when you go thither
limping. Even those who limp go not
backward.

But you who are strong and swift, see
that you do not limp before the lame,
deeming it kindness.

. . .

You are good in countless ways, and you
are not evil when you are not good,

You are only loitering and sluggard.

Pity that the stags cannot teach
swiftness to the turtles.

In your longing for your giant self lies
your goodness: and that longing is in
all of you.

But in some of you that longing is a

torrent rushing with might to the sea,
carrying the secrets of the hillsides
and the songs of the forest.

And in others it is a flat stream that
loses itself in angles and bends and
lingers before it reaches the shore.

But let not him who longs much say to
him who longs little, "Wherefore are
you slow and halting?"

For the truly good ask not the naked,
"Where is your garment?" nor the
houseless, "What has befallen your
house?"

. . . . . .

Then a priestess said, Speak to us
of *Prayer*.

And he answered, saying:

You pray in your distress and in your
need; would that you might pray also
in the fullness of your joy and in your
days of abundance.

For what is prayer but the expansion of
yourself into the living ether?

And if it is for your comfort to pour
your darkness into space, it is also for
your delight to pour forth the dawning
of your heart.

And if you cannot but weep when your
soul summons you to prayer, she should
spur you again and yet again, though
weeping, until you shall come laughing.

When you pray you rise to meet in the air those who are praying at that very hour, and whom save in prayer you may not meet.

Therefore let your visit to that temple invisible be for naught but ecstasy and sweet communion.

For if you should enter the temple for no other purpose than asking you shall not receive:

And if you should enter into it to humble yourself you shall not be lifted:

Or even if you should enter into it to beg for the good of others you shall not be heard.

It is enough that you enter the temple invisible.

. . .

I cannot teach you how to pray in words.

God listens not to your words save when He Himself utters them through your lips.

And I cannot teach you the prayer of the seas and the forests and the mountains. But you who are born of the mountains and the forests and the seas can find their prayer in your heart,

And if you but listen in the stillness of the night you shall hear them saying in silence,

"Our God, who art our winged self, it is

thy will in us that willeth.

It is thy desire in us that desireth.

It is thy urge in us that would turn our nights, which are thine, into days which are thine also.

We cannot ask thee for aught, for thou knowest our needs before they are born in us:

Thou art our need; and in giving us more of thyself thou givest us all."

. . . . . .

Then a hermit, who visited the city once a year, came forth and said, Speak to us of *Pleasure*.

And he answered, saying:

Pleasure is a freedom-song,

But it is not freedom.

It is the blossoming of your desires,

But it is not their fruit.

It is a depth calling unto a height,

But it is not the deep nor the high.

It is the caged taking wing,

But it is not space encompassed.

Ay, in very truth, pleasure is a freedom-song.

And I fain would have you sing it with
fullness of heart; yet I would not have
you lose your hearts in the singing.

Some of your youth seek pleasure as if
it were all, and they are judged and
rebuked. I would not judge nor
rebuke them. I would have them seek.

For they shall find pleasure, but not
her alone;

Seven are her sisters, and the least of
them is more beautiful than pleasure.

Have you not heard of the man who was
digging in the earth for roots and found
a treasure?

. . .

And some of your elders remember
pleasures with regret like wrongs
committed in drunkenness.

But regret is the beclouding of the mind
and not its chastisement.

They should remember their pleasures
with gratitude, as they would the
harvest of a summer.

Yet if it comforts them to regret, let
them be comforted.

And there are among you those who
are neither young to seek nor old to
remember;

And in their fear of seeking and
Remembering they shun all pleasures,
lest they neglect the spirit or offend

against it.

But even in their foregoing is their
pleasure.

And thus they too find a treasure though
they dig for roots with quivering hands.

But tell me, who is he that can offend
the spirit?

Shall the nightingale offend the
stillness of the night, or the firefly
the stars?

And shall your flame or your smoke
burden the wind?

Think you the spirit is a still pool
which you can trouble with a staff?

. . .

Oftentimes in denying yourself pleasure
you do but store the desire in the
recesses of your being.

Who knows but that which seems omitted
today, waits for tomorrow?

Even your body knows its heritage
and its rightful need and will not be
deceived.

And your body is the harp of your soul,

And it is yours to bring forth sweet
music from it or confused sounds.

. . .

And now you ask in your heart, "How

shall we distinguish that which is
good in pleasure from that which is not
good?"

Go to your fields and your gardens, and
you shall learn that it is the pleasure
of the bee to gather honey of the
flower,

But it is also the pleasure of the
flower to yield its honey to the bee.

For to the bee a flower is a fountain of
life,

And to the flower a bee is a messenger
of love,

And to both, bee and flower, the giving
and the receiving of pleasure is a need
and an ecstasy.

People of Orphalese, be in your
pleasures like the flowers and the bees.

. . . . . .

And a poet said, Speak to us of
Beauty.

And he answered:

Where shall you seek beauty, and how
shall you find her unless she herself be
your way and your guide?

And how shall you speak of her except
she be the weaver of your speech?

The aggrieved and the injured say,
"Beauty is kind and gentle.

Like a young mother half-shy of her own
glory she walks among us."

And the passionate say, "Nay, beauty is
a thing of might and dread.

Like the tempest she shakes the earth
beneath us and the sky above us."

The tired and the weary say, "Beauty is
of soft whisperings. She speaks in our
spirit. Her voice yields to our
silences like a faint light that quivers
in fear of the shadow."

But the restless say, "We have heard her
shouting among the mountains,

And with her cries came the sound of
hoofs, and the beating of wings and the
roaring of lions."

At night the watchmen of the city say,
"Beauty shall rise with the dawn from
the east."

And at noontide the toilers and the
wayfarers say, "We have seen her leaning
over the earth from the windows of the
sunset."

. . .

In winter say the snow-bound, "She shall
come with the spring leaping upon the
hills."

And in the summer heat the reapers
say, "We have seen her dancing with the
autumn leaves, and we saw a drift of
snow in her hair." All these things
have you said of beauty,

Yet in truth you spoke not of her but of needs unsatisfied,

And beauty is not a need but an ecstasy.

It is not a mouth thirsting nor an empty hand stretched forth,

But rather a heart enflamed and a soul enchanted.

It is not the image you would see nor the song you would hear,

But rather an image you see though you close your eyes and a song you hear though you shut your ears.

It is not the sap within the furrowed bark, nor a wing attached to a claw,

But rather a garden for ever in bloom and a flock of angels for ever in flight.

. . .

People of Orphalese, beauty is life when life unveils her holy face.

But you are life and you are the veil. Beauty is eternity gazing at itself in a mirror.

But you are eternity and you are the mirror.

. . . . . .

And an old priest said, Speak to us of *Religion.*

And he said:

Have I spoken this day of aught else?

Is not religion all deeds and all
reflection,

And that which is neither deed nor
reflection, but a wonder and a surprise
ever springing in the soul, even while
the hands hew the stone or tend the
loom?

Who can separate his faith from
his actions, or his belief from his
occupations?

Who can spread his hours before him,
saving, "This for God and this for
myself; This for my soul, and this other
for my body?"

All your hours are wings that beat
through space from self to self. He
who wears his morality but as his best
garment were better naked.

The wind and the sun will tear no holes
in his skin.

And he who defines his conduct by ethics
imprisons his song-bird in a cage.

The freest song comes not through bars
and wires.

And he to whom worshipping is a window,
to open but also to shut, has not yet
visited the house of his soul whose
windows are from dawn to dawn.

. . .

Your daily life is your temple and your
religion.

Whenever you enter into it take with you
your all.

Take the plough and the forge and the
mallet and the lute,

The things you have fashioned in
necessity or for delight.

For in revery you cannot rise above your
achievements nor fall lower than your
failures.

And take with you all men: in
adoration you cannot fly higher than
their hopes nor humble yourself lower
than their despair.

. . .

And if you would know God be not
therefore a solver of riddles.

Rather look about you and you shall see
Him playing with your children.

And look into space; you shall see Him
walking in the cloud, outstretching His
arms in the lightning and descending in
rain.

You shall see Him smiling in flowers,
then rising and waving His hands in
trees.

. . . . . .

Then Almitra spoke, saying, We would
ask now of *Death*.

And he said:

You would know the secret of death.

But how shall you find it unless you
seek it in the heart of life?

The owl whose night-bound eyes are blind
unto the day cannot unveil the mystery
of light.

If you would indeed behold the spirit
of death, open your heart wide unto the
body of life.

For life and death are one, even as the
river and the sea are one.

In the depth of your hopes and desires
lies your silent knowledge of the
beyond;

And like seeds dreaming beneath the snow
your heart dreams of spring.

Trust the dreams, for in them is hidden
the gate to eternity. Your fear
of death is but the trembling of the
shepherd when he stands before the king
whose hand is to be laid upon him in
honour.

Is the shepherd not joyful beneath his
trembling, that he shall wear the mark
of the king?

Yet is he not more mindful of his
trembling?

. . .

For what is it to die but to stand naked
in the wind and to melt into the sun?

And what is it to cease breathing, but
to free the breath from its restless
tides, that it may rise and expand and
seek God unencumbered?

Only when you drink from the river of
silence shall you indeed sing.

And when you have reached the mountain
top, then you shall begin to climb.

And when the earth shall claim your
limbs, then shall you truly dance.
And now it was evening.

And Almitra the seeress said, Blessed be
this day and this place and your spirit
that has spoken.

And he answered, Was it I who spoke? Was
I not also a listener?

. . .

Then he descended the steps of the
Temple and all the people followed him.
And he reached his ship and stood upon
the deck.

And facing the people again, he raised
his voice and said:

People of Orphalese, the wind bids me
leave you.

Less hasty am I than the wind, yet I
must go.

We wanderers, ever seeking the lonelier
way, begin no day where we have ended
another day; and no sunrise finds us
where sunset left us. Even while the
earth sleeps we travel.

We are the seeds of the tenacious
plant, and it is in our ripeness and our
fullness of heart that we are given to
the wind and are scattered.

. . .

Brief were my days among you, and
briefer still the words I have spoken.

But should my voice fade in your ears,
and my love vanish in your memory, then
I will come again,

And with a richer heart and lips more
yielding to the spirit will I speak.

Yea, I shall return with the tide,

And though death may hide me, and the
greater silence enfold me, yet again
will I seek your understanding.

And not in vain will I seek.

If aught I have said is truth, that
truth shall reveal itself in a clearer
voice, and in words more kin to your
thoughts.

I go with the wind, people of
Orphalese, but not down into emptiness;
And if this day is not a fulfilment
of your needs and my love, then let it
be a promise till another day.

Man's needs change, but not his love,
nor his desire that his love should
satisfy his needs.

Know therefore, that from the greater
silence I shall return.

The mist that drifts away at dawn,
leaving but dew in the fields, shall
rise and gather into a cloud and then
fall down in rain.

And not unlike the mist have I been.

In the stillness of the night I have
walked in your streets, and my spirit
has entered your houses,

And your heart-beats were in my heart,
and your breath was upon my face, and I
knew you all.

Ay, I knew your joy and your pain,
and in your sleep your dreams were my
dreams.

And oftentimes I was among you a lake
among the mountains.

I mirrored the summits in you and the
bending slopes, and even the
passing flocks of your thoughts and your
desires.

And to my silence came the laughter
of your children in streams, and the
longing of your youths in rivers.

And when they reached my depth the
streams and the rivers ceased not yet to
sing.

But sweeter still than laughter and
greater than longing came to me.

It was the boundless in you;

The vast man in whom you are all but
cells and sinews;

He in whose chant all your singing is
but a soundless throbbing.

It is in the vast man that you are vast,

And in beholding him that I beheld you
and loved you.

For what distances can love reach that
are not in that vast sphere?

What visions, what expectations and what
presumptions can outsoar that flight?

Like a giant oak tree covered with apple
blossoms is the vast man in you. His
might binds you to the earth, his
fragrance lifts you into space, and in
his durability you are deathless.

. . .

You have been told that, even like a
chain, you are as weak as your weakest
link.

This is but half the truth. You are also
as strong as your strongest link.

To measure you by your smallest deed
is to reckon the power of ocean by the
frailty of its foam.

To judge you by your failures is to

cast blame upon the seasons for their
inconstancy.

Ay, you are like an ocean,

And though heavy-grounded ships await
the tide upon your shores, yet, even
like an ocean, you cannot hasten your
tides.

And like the seasons you are also,

And though in your winter you deny your
spring,

Yet spring, reposing within you, smiles
in her drowsiness and is not offended.
Think not I say these things in
order that you may say the one to the
other, "He praised us well. He saw but
the good in us."

I only speak to you in words of that
which you yourselves know in thought.

And what is word knowledge but a shadow
of wordless knowledge?

Your thoughts and my words are waves
from a sealed memory that keeps records
of our yesterdays,

And of the ancient days when the earth
knew not us nor herself,

And of nights when earth was up-wrought
with confusion.

. . .

Wise men have come to you to give you
of their wisdom. I came to take of your

wisdom:

And behold I have found that which is
greater than wisdom.

It is a flame spirit in you ever
gathering more of itself,

While you, heedless of its expansion,
bewail the withering of your days.
It is life in quest of life in
bodies that fear the grave.

. . .

There are no graves here.

These mountains and plains are a cradle
and a stepping-stone.

Whenever you pass by the field where
you have laid your ancestors look well
thereupon, and you shall see yourselves
and your children dancing hand in hand.

Verily you often make merry without
knowing.

Others have come to you to whom for
golden promises made unto your faith
you have given but riches and power and
glory.

Less than a promise have I given, and
yet more generous have you been to me.

You have given me my deeper thirsting
after life.

Surely there is no greater gift to a man
than that which turns all his aims
into parching lips and all life into a

fountain.

And in this lies my honour and my
reward,--

That whenever I come to the fountain
to drink I find the living water itself
thirsty;

And it drinks me while I drink it.

. . .

Some of you have deemed me proud and
over-shy to receive gifts.

Too proud indeed am I to receive wages,
but not gifts.

And though I have eaten berries among
the hills when you would have had me sit
at your board,

And slept in the portico of the temple
when you would gladly have sheltered me,

Yet was it not your loving mindfulness
of my days and my nights that made food
sweet to my mouth and girdled my sleep
with visions?

For this I bless you most:

You give much and know not that you give
at all. Verily the kindness that
gazes upon itself in a mirror turns to
stone,

And a good deed that calls itself by
tender names becomes the parent to a
curse.

. . .

And some of you have called me aloof,
and drunk with my own aloneness,

And you have said, "He holds council
with the trees of the forest, but not
with men.

He sits alone on hill-tops and looks
down upon our city."

True it is that I have climbed the hills
and walked in remote places.

How could I have seen you save from a
great height or a great distance?

How can one be indeed near unless he be
tar?

And others among you called unto me, not
in words, and they said,

"Stranger, stranger, lover of
unreachable heights, why dwell you among
the summits where eagles build
their nests? Why seek you the
unattainable?

What storms would you trap in your net,

And what vaporous birds do you hunt in
the sky?

Come and be one of us.

Descend and appease your hunger with our
bread and quench your thirst with our
wine."

In the solitude of their souls they said

these things;

But were their solitude deeper they
would have known that I sought but the
secret of your joy and your pain,

And I hunted only your larger selves
that walk the sky.

. . .

But the hunter was also the hunted;
For many of my arrows left my bow only
to seek my own breast.

And the flier was also the creeper;
For when my wings were spread in the
sun their shadow upon the earth was a
turtle.

And I the believer was also the doubter;
For often have I put my finger
in my own wound that I might have the
greater belief in you and the greater
knowledge of you.

. . .

And it is with this belief and this
knowledge that I say,

You are not enclosed within your bodies,
nor confined to houses or fields.

That which is you dwells above the
mountain and roves with the wind.

It is not a thing that crawls into
the sun for warmth or digs holes into
darkness for safety,

But a thing free, a spirit that envelops

the earth and moves in the ether.

If these be vague words, then seek not
to clear them.

Vague and nebulous is the beginning of
all things, but not their end,

And I fain would have you remember me as
a beginning.

Life, and all that lives, is conceived
in the mist and not in the crystal.
And who knows but a crystal is mist
in decay?

. . .

This would I have you remember in
remembering me:

That which seems most feeble and
bewildered in you is the strongest and
most determined.

Is it not your breath that has erected
and hardened the structure of your
bones?

And is it not a dream which none of you
remember having dreamt, that built
your city and fashioned all there is in
it?

Could you but see the tides of that
breath you would cease to see all else,

And if you could hear the whispering of
the dream you would hear no other sound.

But you do not see, nor do you hear, and
it is well.

The veil that clouds your eyes shall be lifted by the hands that wove it,

And the clay that fills your ears shall be pierced by those fingers that kneaded it. And you shall see.

And you shall hear.

Yet you shall not deplore having known blindness, nor regret having been deaf.

For in that day you shall know the hidden purposes in all things,

And you shall bless darkness as you would bless light.

After saying these things he looked about him, and he saw the pilot of his ship standing by the helm and gazing now at the full sails and now at the distance.

And he said:

Patient, over patient, is the captain of my ship.

The wind blows, and restless are the sails;

Even the rudder begs direction;

Yet quietly my captain awaits my silence.

And these my mariners, who have heard the choir of the greater sea, they too have heard me patiently. Now they shall wait no longer.

I am ready.

The stream has reached the sea, and
once more the great mother holds her son
against her breast.

. . .

Fare you well, people of Orphalese.

This day has ended.

It is closing upon us even as the
water-lily upon its own tomorrow.

What was given us here we shall keep,

And if it suffices not, then again must
we come together and together stretch
our hands unto the giver.

Forget not that I shall come back to
you.

A little while, and my longing shall
gather dust and foam for another body.

A little while, a moment of rest upon
the wind, and another woman shall bear
me.

Farewell to you and the youth I have
spent with you.

It was but yesterday we met in a
dream. You have sung to me in my
aloneness, and I of your longings have
built a tower in the sky.

But now our sleep has fled and our dream
is over, and it is no longer dawn.

The noontide is upon us and our half
waking has turned to fuller day, and we
must part.

If in the twilight of memory we should
meet once more, we shall speak again
together and you shall sing to me a
deeper song.

And if our hands should meet in another
dream we shall build another tower in
the sky.

. . .

So saying he made a signal to the
seamen, and straightway they weighed
anchor and cast the ship loose from its
moorings, and they moved eastward.

And a cry came from the people as from a single heart, and it rose
into the dusk
and was carried out over the sea like a
great trumpeting.

Only Almitra was silent, gazing after
{the ship until it had vanished into
the mist.

And when all the people were dispersed
she still stood alone upon the sea-wall,
remembering in her heart his saying,

"A little while, a moment of rest upon
the wind, and another woman shall bear
me."

Made in the USA
Middletown, DE
13 August 2021